# MILES·LEWIS
## TOP CHEF

**by Kelly Starling Lyons**
**illustrated by Wayne Spencer**

Penguin Workshop

PENGUIN WORKSHOP
An imprint of Penguin Random House LLC
1745 Broadway, New York, New York 10019

First published in the United States of America by Penguin Workshop,
an imprint of Penguin Random House LLC, 2025

Text copyright © 2025 by Kelly Starling Lyons
Illustrations copyright © 2025 by Penguin Random House LLC

Penguin Random House values and supports copyright. Copyright fuels creativity, encourages diverse voices, promotes free speech, and creates a vibrant culture. Thank you for buying an authorized edition of this book and for complying with copyright laws by not reproducing, scanning, or distributing any part of it in any form without permission. You are supporting writers and allowing Penguin Random House to continue to publish books for every reader. Please note that no part of this book may be used or reproduced in any manner for the purpose of training artificial intelligence technologies or systems.

PENGUIN is a registered trademark and PENGUIN WORKSHOP is a trademark of Penguin Books Ltd, and the W colophon is a registered trademark of Penguin Random House LLC.

Visit us online at penguinrandomhouse.com.

Library of Congress Cataloging-in-Publication Data is available.

Manufactured in China

ISBN 9780593752760 (paperback)          10 9 8 7 6 5 4 3 2 1 TOPL
ISBN 9780593752777 (library binding)     10 9 8 7 6 5 4 3 2 1 TOPL

Design by Mary Claire Cruz and Aya Ghanameh

This book is a work of fiction. Any references to historical events, real people, or real places are used fictitiously. Other names, characters, places, and events are products of the author's imagination, and any resemblance to actual events or places or persons, living or dead, is entirely coincidental.

The authorized representative in the EU for product safety and compliance is Penguin Random House Ireland, Morrison Chambers, 32 Nassau Street, Dublin D02 YH68, Ireland, https://eu-contact.penguin.ie.

For my grandma,
Ruth Starling, whose memory
lives in my heart—KSL

For my wife, Dommie.
You're doing a great job.
Keep it up, but don't forget to
slow down sometimes. Focus on
what's important. The rest will
sort itself out—WS

## CHAPTER ONE

# Master Plan

When it was time for the Flavors of Brookside, my school's bake sale, I knew my family was going to bring it. Each year, I strutted through the door showing off their goodies and cheesing at friends like I was the top chef of the school.

In second grade, Dad made his sweet potato bread. Even my teacher,

Miss Langley, got in line for more. In third grade, Mom made her yummy banana pudding. I helped her add the vanilla wafers and bananas. When the pudding came out of the oven, it looked like a dish on a TV cooking show. As soon as we set the pudding cups down at school, people wanted to gobble them up. I already knew what I wanted to bring this year—Nana's famous tea cakes. They tasted kinda like a cross between sugar cookies and pound cake. Soft and decorated with cinnamon sugar or sprinkles, they were melt-in-your-mouth good. They'd sell out in minutes.

    I couldn't wait to see what everyone else brought. Usually, my school talked about eating healthy. But at the bake sale, every student got a ticket to taste a treat. I always tried something new, like the sandwich cookies called alfajores I loved last year. They had powdered sugar on top and a delicious filling called dulce de leche that tasted kinda like caramel.

Every table in the cafeteria was like a bakery shelf, showing off something different. I didn't know there were so many kinds of brownies, biscuits, and muffins. There were gluten-free treats, too, made with rice flour, in case people had allergies.

"Are you bringing something for the bake sale?" I asked RJ on our bus ride to school.

"What? Huh? I don't know," he said, like he wasn't really listening.

I knew something was up.

"What's wrong?"

"Nothing."

RJ looked out the window. It wasn't like him to not talk. I hoped he would tell me what was bothering him, but I didn't push it. He would share when he was ready.

When we pulled up at Brookside, I thought of something that could bring RJ out of his funk.

"Want to play basketball after school?"

RJ shook his head.

Now, I knew something was wrong.

"You never turn down a chance to hoop. What's going on?"

He sighed.

"I broke my mom's keepsake box. She always tells me not to dribble in the house. I just did it a little. But I bumped into her special wooden box and broke it. What am I going to do?"

"Whoa. That's tough. Why don't

you just tell her what happened? I bet Miss Nikki will understand."

"That box came from my grandpa."

He put his head down.

RJ didn't have to say anything else. I knew what breaking a box from his grandpa meant. He lived across the country in Oklahoma and just had surgery on his leg. Miss Nikki flew out there to help as he recovered. Gifts from his grandpa meant a lot.

We walked to class in silence. Our desks were next to each other. RJ usually joked around until it was time to get to work. This time, he didn't say a word.

When Miss Taylor hit the chime for our morning meeting, we headed for the orange-and-blue carpet.

"We're going to do a special project," she said and grinned.

Friends whispered to each other, trying to guess what it could be.

"Who likes to bake?"

Hands shot up. I shrugged. I liked to help Nana when she baked. But the last time I tried to bake something on my own, even I didn't want to eat it.

"This week, we're going to learn the connections between chemistry and baking."

I leaned in to make sure I heard her right. Chemistry? That was the key? I smiled and relaxed. Now, that was more like it.

"And I have great news. A local bakery is sponsoring a writing contest and a baking contest for students at our school this year. You can write an essay about your favorite food. Or you can bake something and bring it in for the Flavors of Brookside. The top prize

for each contest is a hundred dollars. If you want an entry form, let me know."

RJ stood up and raised his hand when she mentioned money.

"I have two questions: Can you enter both contests? Also, can you work in a team for the bake sale?"

"Sure. You can only win one prize, but you can enter both. If you want to have what you make judged for the bakery contest, you can work with a friend. You just can't have an adult do it for you."

RJ looked at me. I looked at him. I could see his mind working. After the morning meeting, he got the entry forms from Miss Taylor.

"I know what to do," RJ said, clutching the papers. "I can buy Mom a new box that's just like the old one. My big cousin helped me look it up. It costs forty-five dollars. I *have* to win one of those contests."

"I don't know, RJ. I still think you

should tell Miss Nikki when she gets back."

He made a sour face and shook his head.

"She's already worried about my grandpa. I just want to get her a new box. You always bring the best stuff for the bake sale. Can you help me make something good?"

My stomach rocked like I was riding a roller coaster. I wanted to help RJ. But was it okay to pretend a new box was the one his grandpa gave his mom? I wasn't sure.

RJ's eyes pleaded with me to say yes. I nodded and told myself to stop worrying.

"I'm in."

Now how could we win that prize? I stared into space like the answer was there. What did I get myself into? Then, it came to me! Instead of asking Nana to make tea cakes, RJ and I could make them together. I had flopped at baking before. But now we had a secret weapon—science. What could go wrong?

## CHAPTER TWO
# Special Ingredient

**W**hen I got home from school, Nana was waiting for me like always. She was sitting in the dining room, working on a project. Colorful squares of cloth stretched across the table like a rainbow.

"Hey, Miles," she said, grabbing a square and sewing it onto another one. "How was school?"

"It was good," I said, kissing her on the cheek. "What are you working on?"

"Guess."

I looked closely and realized the squares weren't just random pieces of fabric. A blue striped print with a "5" in the middle reminded me of a shirt I used to love when I was little.

"Is that my old birthday shirt?"

"Sure is."

Suddenly, I knew just what she was doing. I had seen her work on one when my aunt had a baby.

"You're making a quilt!"

"Bingo. A family quilt, pieces of us stitched together. Shows that we're united no matter where we are."

The more I looked at the squares, the more I remembered about where they came from. There was a piece of my cousin Cam's tie-dye shirt from his favorite summer camp. There was a chunk of black and gold that looked like it came from one of my mom's old Steelers jerseys. There was my dad's orange-and-white checked dress shirt. He joked that he was going to retire it because he had it so long. I guess Nana had another idea.

"That's so cool," I said.

"Maybe you can help me put some of the quilt together."

"Count me in!"

That reminded me of something I needed her help with.

"We're learning about baking and chemistry at school."

Nana nodded her head while starting to stitch on another patch.

"Miss Taylor said we can enter a baking contest, too. RJ and I are going to work together. I was thinking we could make your tea cakes."

Nana paused and looked at me like she was amused.

"*My* tea cakes," she said, grinning. "Don't you mean *your* tea cakes? I think you love them more than anyone in the house."

We laughed. She had a point. But I always helped her make them. I never made them on my own. What if I messed up?

I filled Nana in on the rules of the contest.

"Do you think you could give us some tips?"

"Sure," she said. "I can't do it for you since you're supposed to do it independently. But I'll share what works for me."

I grinned and got ready to do my homework. With science and coaching from Nana, RJ would be out of his jam in no time. We had this contest in the bag.

When Mom and Dad got home from the university where they worked, I told them about my big plan.

"I'm proud of you, Miles," Mom said, patting my shoulder. "I tried to make your nana's tea cakes once, and they just didn't turn out like hers."

"Yeah," Dad said. "Your nana always seems to leave out part of the recipe. Isn't that right?"

He winked at her.

"Well, you know I don't really use recipes," Nana said. "But when I write out how I make things, I try to include as much detail as I can. But it's more than following directions that makes tea cakes special."

More than following directions? Uh-oh. That queasy roller-coaster feeling was back. Maybe this was trickier than I thought.

"You know Nana isn't the only expert at baking," Dad said. "Remember when we went to Mama Dip's Kitchen in Chapel Hill?"

I smiled and nodded. How could I forget that awesome restaurant? The menu had fried pickles and sweet potato biscuits. Everything was delicious. Dad told me lots of famous people had eaten there, even basketball hero Michael Jordan and tennis star Venus Williams. I couldn't believe my parents even met Mama Dip before she died years ago.

"Mama Dip is part of a tradition of Black cooks and chefs. Let's look her up and learn more."

I knew that was coming. Dad teaches Black history. He loves dropping what he calls "pearls of knowledge."

I put Mama Dip's name

into a search on the computer. Lots of results came up. I learned that her real name was Mildred Council and she learned to cook by watching her family. Years after her mom died, she became the main cook in her house. She was just nine, the same age as me. I read that when Mama Dip got older, she called herself a "dump cook" because she didn't measure her ingredients. She figured out the right measurements by how things felt, looked, and tasted. Maybe that was the something special Nana was talking about. I looked away from the screen. Cooking without measuring? I couldn't do that. RJ was counting on me. What if I let him down?

"What's wrong, Miles?" Dad asked.

"Nana and Mama Dip know how to cook by heart. They don't even use recipes. How am I supposed to do that?"

"When I bake, I make sure everything is measured just right," he said. "That's how a lot of people do it. Following directions is important. But sometimes you can add your own flavor, too. You have to find the way that works best for you."

Dad put his hand on my shoulder to let me know he cared. What he said made sense. I hoped RJ and I could figure out the recipe for success.

## CHAPTER THREE

# The Science of Cooking

On the bus the next day, RJ got right to business.

"I started working on my essay," he said, settling into the seat next to me. "I'm writing about the buffalo chicken dip my family makes on movie nights. Now, we just have to figure out what we're going to bake."

"How about my nana's tea cakes?"

RJ grinned like it was time for recess.

"Yes!" he said and pulled down his fist like he just scored a goal. "Your nana's cookies are so good. We'll definitely win that prize."

Sitting across the aisle from us, Kyla overheard what he said and chimed in.

"I don't know about that," she said, twisting her lips. "Gabi is making something special. Aren't you, Gabi?"

Gabi nodded.

"I'm making tres leches cake," she said. "My abuela taught me how to make it."

"Yum," Jada said. "I had a piece at your birthday party. Can't wait to have another one. I'm making soft pretzels."

Uh-oh. I had one of those when I visited Jada's house. It was so good. This would be harder than I thought.

All this talk about the bake sale filled my mind with doubts. What if what RJ and I made was a fail? What if someone else won? I turned to talk to RJ. There was still time for him to tell his mom the truth. Then, we could just enter the contest for fun.

It was like he was reading my mind.

"Don't worry," RJ said. "Your nana's tea cakes will win the top prize."

Then he added softly, "They have to."

I looked out the window so RJ

didn't see my frown. I wished there was another way to help.

At science time, Miss Taylor had a fun experiment set up for us. There were stations around the room with plastic bowls, measuring spoons, and labeled clear cups.

"Every ingredient you use in baking has a job to do," she said. "Today, we're doing experiments with baking powder and baking soda so we can learn how they help make our food rise. Anyone know some differences between them?"

I had seen Nana use both. But I wasn't sure when it was time to

use one or the other. Seemed like everyone else was confused, too.

"Well, we're going to see how they work firsthand," Miss Taylor said. "You and your partner are going to take turns mixing water with each substance and then mixing them with vinegar. Write down the results. Then, we'll discuss what happened."

Miss Taylor called out the partners. Jada and I were a team. I smiled. We both collected rocks and loved kitchen chemistry. Science was our thing.

Jada measured a tablespoon of baking powder into the bowl and stirred in water from one of the cups.

"Look at that!" she said as it began

to softly fizz. Usually, I'd be excited about a reaction like that. But I just nodded.

Next, it was my turn. I mixed baking soda with water. Figured—no fizz for me. All it did was turn the water cloudy.

After we wrote down the results,

Jada asked if I wanted to go first with the vinegar.

"No, you can do it."

I was passing up the chance to discover something new. Jada studied me and scrunched her eyebrows.

"Are you okay, Miles?"

"I don't know," I said, leaning my cheek against my fist. "I thought

learning about baking and chemistry would be cool. But RJ keeps talking about the bake sale. He really wants to win. What if we don't? I don't know what to do."

"You know RJ always likes to compete," Jada said. "It doesn't matter who wins. Just have fun."

"RJ needs the money for something important."

"Oh."

She was quiet for a while like she was searching for a solution.

"Well, my mom says to 'Think positive,'" she said. "Just do your best. It will work out."

I wanted to believe her. I had heard my mom say the same thing. Jada scooped some baking soda into the bowl. Then, she held out the cup of vinegar.

"You sure you don't want to go first?" she said, pretending like she was going to pour it.

"Wait a minute! I'll do it."

Jada laughed because she knew that would get me.

I took the cup and stirred in the vinegar. Not only did the mixture

fizz, but the bubbles foamed and rose.

"Now, that's a reaction!" Jada said.

She was up next. When Jada mixed the vinegar with the baking powder, I thought we would see something different.

"Wow!" we both said at the same time.

Jada made bubbles rise in the bowl, too. You never knew what was going to happen until you tried. Sometimes different methods got similar results.

↯ *CHAPTER FOUR* ↯

# Chefs in Training

On Saturday, RJ's dad dropped him off so we could start baking.

"Hey, RJ!" Nana said, giving him a hug when he came into the house.

We followed Nana into the dining room where we had been cutting old clothes into squares of fabric.

"Let's put this up and then we can get started in the kitchen."

RJ looked at the clothing, fabric squares, scissors, mat, and sewing tools.

"What are you making, Mrs. Lewis?"

"A family quilt," she said. "There's a piece of each of us in this."

"That's my shirt from my favorite birthday party," I said, pointing to the blue square. "That's a piece from one of my granddad's jackets."

"That's really cool," RJ said.

"Thanks," Nana said. "Miles has been helping me this morning. Want to cut out a square before I put it up?"

"Sure!"

She showed RJ how to measure the fabric, draw a light line as a guide so he got the size right, and cut out a square.

"Great job!" she said. "I think I'll add that piece right here."

It was near the center of a row she was working on.

RJ smiled.

"Miles told me your grandpa had surgery. How's he doing?"

"Mom said that he'll be healing for a while. But he's feeling a little better. She and my grandma have been taking good care of him. Mom will be back next week, right after the bake sale."

"That's good," she said. "Real good."

As we helped Nana put everything into her sewing basket, I looked at the patterns she created on the quilt. With squares and triangles of clothing and other fabric, she was telling our story. She planned to embroider our names on the bottom when she was finished. It was kind of like the keepsake box that RJ broke of his mom's. It was special, something that couldn't be replaced. I started wondering again if it was okay for RJ to just buy his mom a new box. Something kept telling me that it wasn't right.

"Okay, who's ready to bake?" Nana asked.

"I'm ready to win that contest," RJ said, grinning like he already knew we would come in first.

"I don't know about all that," Nana

said. "My tea cakes are good. But other people have specialties, too. All I can do is give you some pointers."

In the kitchen with Nana, the first thing you did was wash your hands. Next, Nana handed us a sheet of paper with her recipe written on it. I looked it over. I had messed up making cookies before. But this time would be different. Miss Taylor taught us how different ingredients helped with baking. That science knowledge would come in handy. I even had experience rolling out the dough and adding the sprinkles from helping Nana in the past. I was ready to rock this challenge.

"Okay, Miles, what do you do first?" Nana asked, quizzing to see if I remembered.

"Gather what we need."

RJ and I looked in the fridge and the cabinets for the ingredients: butter, flour, sugar, vanilla, cinnamon, sprinkles, baking powder, salt, and eggs. Looks like we had everything.

"Okay, here are a few tips," she said. "Take your time and make sure you add each ingredient the way it says. The batter can get really sticky. Flour the board and your hands so it's easier to work with. When you're ready to put the tea cakes in the oven, let me know. I'll be there to do that part."

She sat in our living room, which was next to the kitchen, and flipped through a magazine so we could work alone.

"First prize, here we come!" RJ said.

Nana had left the sticks of butter out to soften. We added them to a bowl and mixed them with the sugar until they were blended into a sunshine-yellow cream. I had to sneak a taste. RJ did, too.

"You boys might want to leave some for the tea cakes," Nana said playfully.

Caught. I didn't know she was looking.

Next, RJ and I took turns cracking the eggs. I got a little piece of shell inside the bowl.

"Let an expert show you how it's done," RJ joked as I fished it out.

But when it was his turn, he got some in, too.

"Looks like I'm not the only one who needs some practice."

We laughed, got it out, and kept going.

Next, it was time for the dry ingredients. We started by adding flour to another bowl. I couldn't find the one-cup scoop, so we used half

cups. Flour flew everywhere as we dipped the measuring cup into the container and dumped it into the bowl. It was on our clothes and the counter. I lost count of how many scoops we put in.

"How many more do we need, RJ?"

"I thought you were keeping count."

"I thought you were."

I looked at Nana. She looked down at her magazine. This was for us to figure out.

"I think we're good," RJ said.

I hoped so. We added the last few ingredients and mixed everything together. The batter seemed like a different texture than when Nana makes it. But maybe I wasn't remembering right. We rolled out the dough, cut it into circles, and put them on the greased cookie sheet. We sprinkled some with cinnamon sugar and others with cinnamon. They looked good.

"We're ready, Nana."

She showed us how to set the timer. Then, she slid the tea cakes into the oven. Before we knew it, the timer buzzed.

"I smell tea cakes," Mom said, coming into the kitchen with my dad. "Enough for us to try?"

"Sure!" RJ said. "Get ready for the winning recipe."

They looked flatter than usual when Nana took them out of the oven. I got a funny feeling that something wasn't right. After they cooled, Daddy had the first bite. Crunch. Ugh. I flinched. Nana's tea cakes are soft.

"Not bad," Daddy said, chewing

longer than he should have to. "Keep going. You'll get it."

My mom tasted one next. She tried to keep a cheerful face, but I could tell they weren't her favorite.

When RJ and I tried them, I knew we had messed up.

"These don't taste like your nana's," RJ said, frowning.

"I don't know what we did wrong."

"It was just your first try," Nana said, comforting us. "Let's go back through your steps. Did you add everything?"

As I looked through the ingredients, I noticed the baking powder container on the floor. I picked it up.

"We forgot to put this in! It must have fallen and we didn't notice. That's why the tea cakes look so flat."

"You should have seen me when I started baking," Nana said to us, laughing. "My cookies could have been paperweights, they were so heavy. Go ahead and get ready for round two. I'll be right back."

RJ and I started adding ingredients for a new batch, but everything we did got on each other's nerves. We bickered over who was adding what first and if we were stirring right.

I had enough.

"Why can't you just tell your mom what happened? This isn't working."

"I can't," he said. "If you were really my friend, you'd try harder."

"Even if we win, the new box won't be the same. It's not the one your grandpa gave her."

I could see the hurt in RJ's eyes. When Nana came back in, he walked over to her.

"Mrs. Lewis, I'm ready to go home."

She looked at me to see what was going on. I put my head down.

"Okay, RJ, let me get my keys. I'll drive you."

I couldn't believe what had happened. I just wanted to forget about the contest—nothing about this was fun.

## CHAPTER FIVE

# Crunch Time

Our first day together in the kitchen was a flop. We just had a few days left before the bake sale. What were we going to do?

On the bus, RJ and I sat in different seats. When I caught him staring at me, he looked away. At school, RJ rushed down the hall. I tried to catch up to him, but Carson wanted to ask me something. I saw

RJ walk into our class and wondered how long he was going to be mad at me.

At morning meeting, we didn't sit next to each other like we usually do. When we got back to our desks, I leaned over to him.

"I'm sorry for what I said."

RJ nodded. But he didn't look me in the eye. Later, at snack time, he came over and sat next to me on the carpet.

"You were right, Miles," he said. "I haven't been feeling good about not telling my mom, either. I still want to buy her another box. But I have to tell her what I did."

Whew. I was glad RJ was going to be honest. I knew it was hard to admit when you did something wrong.

"When we win the contest, I can buy her the box. Then, when she gets home, I'll tell her what I did and give her the new one. Maybe it won't be so bad."

"Maybe," I said. "But what if we don't win?"

He didn't have an answer for that.

We planned another baking day at my house. This one would be for real. Whatever we made is what we would enter in the contest. My mom, dad, and nana had already talked to me about being a good friend. They didn't know why RJ left but could tell he was hurt.

I was ready to try again if he was.

    The next day, we got off the bus together and walked to my house.

    "Time for a do-over?" Nana asked when we came in. She hugged us both.

"You two are friends," she said. "Put some of that good feeling into your baking. Miles, you know how your dad says I have a secret ingredient. I'm ready to tell you what it is. Come close, boys."

She said it softly like it was a secret: "Always add some love."

We made the tea cakes again. This time, we followed the directions and worked together. I thought about the science of baking and how every ingredient had a job to do. I trusted my instincts, too, splashing in a little extra vanilla and an extra shake of cinnamon. Maybe Dad was right. You could add your own flavor.

When Nana took the tea cakes out of the oven, RJ and I tasted them first. Yum. We did it! They came out just right.

Nana clapped and nodded her head when she saw our smiles.

"Mom! Dad!" I called. "The tea cakes are ready!"

I didn't have to tell them again. They rushed right in. It was like they knew we got it this time.

"Now, this is what I'm talking about," Mom said, closing her eyes as she savored the taste.

"You're giving Nana a run for her money," Dad said.

Maybe we had a shot at winning after all.

## CHAPTER SIX

# Recipe for Success

**B**efore I entered the cafeteria for the Flavors of Brookside, I could tell that the competition was going to be tough. Sweet, spicy, and tangy smells made my stomach grumble. Inside, I saw tables full of rolls, muffins, dessert bars, cakes, biscuits, and pies. Essays mounted on colorful paper hung on the walls. One was about samosas. Another was about beef patties and coco bread. I loved reading about all the food my school friends enjoyed.

Just then, I saw RJ. He looked upset.

"My dad said my mom got back early. She's getting ready to come to the bake sale. She'll be here soon."

"That's okay. You're going to tell her, right?"

"Yeah, but I thought I had more time."

The bakery judges walked around tasting the food made by the students. We nudged each other when they ate our tea cakes.

"Maybe it will still work out," RJ said. "I think they liked them."

I couldn't tell what they thought. Seemed like they smiled and nodded each time they tasted something new.

I saw RJ's mom and dad before he did.

"Your parents are here," I whispered to him.

RJ turned their way and smiled, but it didn't look real. His mouth was grinning, but his eyes were cloudy like the sky before it pours.

"Can you come over with me?"

His mom held out her arms and gave RJ a big hug.

"Heard you two have been

working hard. Can't wait to taste what you made."

RJ looked at her and took a breath.

"Mom, I need to tell you something."

Every second felt like an hour.

"I broke your special keepsake box, the one Grandpa gave you," he finally said. "I'm really sorry. I'm going to buy you another one if Miles and I win the prize money. But I know it won't be the same as the one you had before."

At first, his mom was silent as a stone. Her face was blank like she was taking in what he just said. Then, she hugged him again.

"Thank you for being honest," she said. "Accidents happen. What matters is that you apologize and own up to what you did."

"You're not mad?"

"No. I'm proud of you. I could tell it was hard for you to share what happened, but you told me. That keepsake box was special. But I have other treasures from your grandpa and the best keepsakes are the memories I hold in my heart."

RJ smiled, a real one this time. I did, too.

I saw Jada, Kyla, and Gabi.

"Hey, RJ and Miles," Jada said.

"Want to walk around together?"

"You and Miles go and have fun," Miss Nikki said to RJ.

We hung out with our friends, tasting treats and laughing. Then, it was time for the contest results. The crowd hushed as Mrs. Keane, our assistant principal, got ready to make the announcement.

"Everybody did an amazing job," she said. "You're all winners. First prize for the bake sale goes to Gabi Rodriguez for her tres leches cake."

We cheered. I knew what I was using my ticket for—I was definitely trying a piece of that. First prize for the essay went to Kevin Thurman. He was a third grader who wrote about

making homemade pepperoni pizza with his family.

I looked at RJ to see if he was disappointed. He turned to me and frowned. Uh-oh.

"Just kidding," he said, grinning. "This was awesome. I was thinking about doing something different for my mom since we didn't win the contest. Do you think your nana would show me how to make a quilt? Maybe I can get some of my grandparents' clothes the next time we go to Oklahoma."

"Did someone say quilt?"

Nana was behind us. How did she do that? She always showed up at just the right time.

"Of course, RJ. You can come over this weekend if it's okay with your mom and dad."

He scrunched his eyebrows like he was thinking something over.

"Miles, what do you think about us making a quilt together?"

"I thought you were making it with your family."

"I am, but you and I could make our own. Friends are family, too."

I loved that.

"What if we make a friendship quilt?" I said. "We could add pieces of clothes from you and me, Jada, Carson, Gabi, Lena, Kyla, and Simone. Maybe Miss Taylor will let us do it for a class project so everyone can be part of it."

Turns out the recipe for success wasn't food at all. It was in our hearts all along.

# Miles's Five Facts

**My dad loves dropping Black history facts. He thinks it's great to learn more about people who paved the way for us.**

**Here are a few things I learned. Did you know:**

*1.* **Though he was enslaved for more than thirty years, James Hemings was the first American to train in Paris as a chef. He made macaroni and cheese and ice cream popular in the US by putting his twist on French versions. People loved it.**

2. One of the top Southern chefs was Edna Lewis. She learned to cook on a farm when she was little. She grew up to be a famous chef who wrote cookbooks and even made food for important people like First Lady Eleanor Roosevelt.

3. Mama Dip was the nickname of Mildred Council, who grew up in Chatham County, North Carolina. Her daddy taught her and her siblings how to cook. Her restaurant opened more than forty years ago in the North Carolina Triangle, where I live.

4. Have you ever been to the National Museum of African American History and Culture in Washington, DC? There's a cool dining hall there called the Sweet Home Café. Chef Carla Hall was the culinary ambassador when it opened in 2016.

5. Tea cakes, my favorite dessert, don't need a lot of ingredients. But always remember Nana's secret ingredient: Add some love.

# Acknowledgments

Some keepsakes in my family have been handed down—recipes, photos, plates, quilts. They are priceless and full of meaning. But the best keepsakes are the memories I hold in my heart. I was thinking about that when I came up with this story. RJ broke a box that meant a lot to his mom. He worries about getting in trouble and letting her down. Does he tell the truth or cover it up? Does Miles go along with his decision even if he feels it may be wrong?

You're going to face tough decisions just like RJ and Miles. You know in your heart what's best. Trust that instinct, be brave, and believe in yourself. I believe in you. If you make a mistake, try to own it and correct it. Messing up is part of life. It's always the right time to make a better choice. Stand tall and know you matter, and you're loved.

Thank you to my amazing editor Renee Kelly, to gifted illustrator Wayne Spencer, to the all-star Penguin Workshop team, to my wonderful agent, Caryn, and to my mom and to my friend Judy Allen Dodson for their feedback on this story. I also want to thank my grandparents, mom, father, children, aunts, uncles, and cousins for the memories and support. You are part of me always.

As a kid, I helped my grandma make tea cakes just like Miles. Want to make some of your own? Visit the Miles Lewis section of my website (www.kellystarlinglyons.com) for my recipe.

# Want more Miles? Find him in the Jada Jones series!